Dedicated to: All the people that inspired this book. I would like to say hallelujah to my editor because I think I learned to spell a few unfamiliar words! Thank you. Last but not least my father, Richard A. Perry, has passed on but still lives in my heart. Thanks, Y'all!

-Josie Ann Tyler

Hairdresser Of Oz

Family of Oz series, Volume 3

Josie Ann Tyler

Published by Josie Ann TYler, 2023.

HAIRDRESSER OF OZ

First edition. April 17, 2023.

Copyright © 2023 Josie Ann Tyler.

ISBN: 979-8215127285

Written by Josie Ann Tyler.

Chapter 1

I just finished up my chores as I was coming inside to start on my homework.

But Mom stopped me in the living room "I want you to clean up your bedroom then you can start on your homework."

That's one thing about being homeschooled: you can do your homework any time of the day.

Mom was getting ready to leave to go into town to the shop she worked at. She was the manager. She had an order of 200 bars of goat's milk soap to make in less than 3 weeks.

I hated cleaning my room. It was like a death sentence. I would like to do anything but this!

It wouldn't help much when your sister Blair would not help clean her part of the room and was in the living room.

As I was cleaning my room, I found my ultimate junior hair accessory kit. It was under my bunk bed.

"Now how did it get there?" I was finding more hair stuff that I had not seen in months.

After finding everything, I went into the living room and told Blair and Josie what I found. Let's do our hair and color it as well.

We didn't know we were in the bathroom that long and Albert was just getting home from work and needed to use the bathroom. He always came home at the most inopportune times. When he got done, we all went back in and colored our hair. I was coloring the ends of my hair a light rose pink when out of nowhere we all saw a butterfly barrette flying toward me. It landed on the top of my head. It gave me the heebie-jeebies. I'm not a particular fan of any bugs. I was trying to get the barrette out, but it was like it was super-glued to my hair.

"No problem Abby, I can get it out," Blair told me. She worked and worked at it but the barrette would not budge. Josie, ever the confident one of the bunch said, "Move over. I can get it out better than you guys. My hair is curly, I have to get things like this out of my hair all the time."

Blair and I looked at each other with an expression that said 'Here we go again'.

Josie grabbed the coconut oil and put it around where the barrette was and pulled on it.

"Ouch!! Would you watch what you are doing!"

Then out of nowhere, there was a flash of light and I was gone. Josie and Blair were freaking out and didn't know what to do.

They were both scared and just stood in awe; they did not know Larry was standing there. He looked around and started calling for Frederick and Darla. They came running and told them what happened.

Larry yelled, " We missed the rapture!"

Josie said, "I guess we did not listen to Mom." She always said children obey their parents in everything and that is what the bible said."

Blair ran to see if Albert was still sleeping, but he was not there. Blair screamed at the top of her lungs, "You guys will not believe that Albert is not here either!!!!!"

Larry ran out of the house, but Albert's car was still there. They did not know he went for a walk up to cougars and bear country.

Josie called Mom but no answer. She came in to see if Tammy was there, but she was not as well. They all cried.

Josie tried calling Dad but no answer. She called Stephanie, their sister-in-law, but still no answer. She tried everybody she knew, but no one answered. Josie yelled to the kids to stay inside. "I'm going to see if the neighbors are home." She went to the next-door neighbor's house, but they were not there. She went to Lisa, the lady that lived across the road, but she wasn't there either.

As Josie was going around looking for anyone that was still home, Albert walked into the house and when he did all go the kids that were in the house ran up to him and told him all that had just happened.

Albert replied, "Where have you been, open your eyes. This is the third time that someone has mysteriously gone missing. Don't you get the drift? She most likely went to Oz. Duh!"

Then Josie walked into the house and told them that there were no neighbors home and that she had called everyone that she knew and they didn't answer either. "Dadgummit even Tammy is gone!!"

"Well, I can answer some of your questions. Mrs. K took Tammy to the library, so that's where she is, and your mom is at the shop making soap and she probably turned off her phone so she didn't have to listen to your complaints. Don't you guys ever think things through? There is this wonderful thing called context clues. Maybe you should call again," Albert said.

Blair got annoyed "Now who's the one who isn't thinking? You can't have your cell phone on in the library."

Chapter 2

Meanwhile, all that was happening I was being taken away by that weird butterfly barrette thing. "Put me down!" I yelled. Well, that shows what I know. The butterfly kept flying and flying until it came to a meadow of many types of butterflies flying about.

Just then, the butterfly barrette dropped me in mid-air. I kept falling thinking. I was going for so long that I thought I was never going to stop.

This day is not going the way I planned it, she thought. With a thump, she landed on her back in a pile of wet leaves.

Sitting up, she was engulfed in butterflies all over herself. I sneezed so loudly it made the butterflies flutter away. Finally.

"Well now, what am I going to do, and which way do I go from here? Larry and Josie both said they had to go to Emerald City and get help from the Lion, Tinman, and also the Scarecrow."

So, standing up, she checked out her surroundings to see which way to go, and hopefully, that would be the right way and it would not take so long to get back home as Larry and Josie did.

Well, I guess this way is better than no way at all, so I went straight. Just my luck, I was supposed to be going to a summer camp tomorrow.

I hope it will not upset Mom because I left the house when she always said to stay inside when she is not home unless she told us to go outside to take care of something on the farm. Like, check on an animal or something like that.

Looking around, there was not much to see. All I saw was wheat fields after wheat fields. Boy does this get old soon. Will I ever get done with being in a wheat field?

This was one of the most boring days of my life. I need to get out of this area.

If I can just get home, I will always keep my room clean. Please send me home now. I do not want to be walking and walking for days and days, I prayed to God.

I heard lots of cars and people yelling. This reminded me of watching FASCAR. Also on the other side, there were RVs. I thought I might as well sit down a while and watch a little excitement while I was here. I was kinda bored anyway.

I found a stump to sit on and I finished watching the car races. It took a good part of the day away from my walk, but I never got to see a car race before.

By the time the race was over the sun was setting and it was time to plan where I would sleep for the night. I remember behind me was a blackberry bush and a pretty good size hole. I could sleep inside the hole. So I crawled through the hole in the middle of the bushes. It had lots of straw, so I started picking up the straw and made a place for me to lie on. It was better than sleeping on the cold ground, that's for sure.

Chapter 3

I woke up to two skunks looking at me. I crawled off the hay and back through the hole until I could not see them anymore.

I sure was lucky back there. Those skunks could have sprayed me and I don't have any tomato juice so I would have to smell the entire way to the Emerald City. With me smelling like that they'll never let me in when I go to ask for help. That would be pretty unfortunate.

I sure hope I have better luck than this. I was wondering what my family was doing at home at that moment. At the same time I was thinking that I heard a loud thunderclap and looking up at the sky I saw a person on a glider. The glider was not like any other glider that I had ever seen and it was kind of fascinating. It had one wheel in the front and two in the back. It had a seat that was in the middle of the thing and it kinda reminded me of a motorbike.

The glider was coming in for a landing. As it was getting to the ground, I got a better view of the person in the contraption. It was a girl with long, red, wavy hair. She had a black skirt and a black shirt on. She noticed me right away.

When she got closer enough that I could see more of her features I saw that she had the bluest eyes that I had ever seen.

When she said hello to me, her voice was creepy. It sounded like someone scraping their fingernails across the blackboard. At first, the way she talked puzzled me. I finally had enough courage to say "Hello"

She looked like a teenager, but I was not sure as she talked. I just wish she would shut up.

"I never saw you around these parts before."

At first, I was not sure if I should tell her, but I decided to.

"I'm not from around here I'm from Lebanon, Oregon"

She just stared at me and asked, "How did you get here?"

I explained how I got here and she looked at me like she didn't believe me.

"Are you a witch?"

"Why do you say that?"

"Because of how you said you got here."

Thinking to myself, should I also ask her if she is a witch as well?

"Are you a witch?"

"Why yes, I am. What do you think all witches are ugly?"

I didn't have an answer to this. I just looked at her blankly.

The young witch said, "Be gone, with you, or I will go get my grandmother, the witch from the black hole. I could not believe what I heard. This must be the same old lady that Josie said lived in the black hole of Oz. Without another word, I just walked on by and kept going without turning back.

As I got closer to the next town, I could smell coffee. I saw the sign of the town. It read "Brewerville, where you'll always be awake" I wonder what they drink here.

What I saw so far was coffee shops handing out free coffee samples.

I wish I had enough money to buy a caramel mocha latte that would be so good.

As I was walking along the sidewalk I noticed that there was some money on the ground. I didn't see anyone around and so I went ahead and bent down and grabbed the money. I then continued to walk around town. I finally figured out that they were a coffee town, this Brewerville.

Before long I saw a sign that read

Half Off All Caramel Mocha Lattes. Today Only

I looked around to see if anyone was following me. I still wasn't sure if anyone had seen me pick up the money. I kept debating within myself if I should use the money to buy a mocha latte or if I should go find a cop and give it to him to return to whoever it belonged to.

But a little voice in the back of my mind kept telling me that it was ok to use the money and so I decided that no one was going to miss the money and I went inside the cafe to get a latte.

I went and stood in the line. I guess no one wants a caramel mocha latte today. Even though they are half off. There was hardly anyone there.

I was next in line. The man smiled at me, "How can I help you?"

"I would like a large caramel mocha latte please."

I walked over to the pickup line and waited behind a tall man.

When I picked up my latte I just held it in my hand because it was so warm. Finding a seat was nearly impossible. I found a small round table in the corner by the front window. I sat there by the window sipping my coffee and watching all of the busy people in the town.

I thought to myself, *this must be a pretty busy town. Do they only sell coffee drinks? I guess they do because their sign says well always be awake.*

As I was walking out of the coffee shop, I looked up and saw the name of the coffee shop: Abigail's coffee shop. It shares my name. A big smile came across my face and I went on my way.

Down the sidewalk a bit, a man was handing out free samples of coffee. He offered me one sample to me.

This one was a peppermint mocha. Oh, I love mochas. If only my brothers and sister could see me now.

Down another block, they were giving out samples of strawberry scones. They were delicious. This town smelled so good.

Over in a field, I saw a factory and smoke was coming out of the chimney. You could smell the making of coffee.

This is one town I would like to have a second home in. Maybe when I get to Emerald City, I can ask if I can have a home here as well. Wouldn't that be a joy?

I was at the end of the town when I noticed that there was a little clothing store. *Haha, I guess coffee isn't all they sell here,* I thought.

Chapter 4

Just as I was out of town, I saw a sign that said,

Thank you for staying awake in our town. Come again!!

I looked over to the other side, and the sign said,

Welcome to Brewerville. Come on in and always stay awake!!

Now that I was out of town I felt bad for using the money I had gotten on the sidewalk. I felt like I should have gone to the sheriff and seen if anyone was missing any money. Although there was no wallet. But on the other hand, I could have gotten an envelope and put it somewhere where someone could find it. I'm sure I could have lived without the caffeine. I thought, what would Mom and Dad do if they had found the money? I tried to stop thinking about it as I was walking but it wouldn't shake.

I just had to find something different to think about. It was a nice spring day with the birds flying about.

I was wondering how far it would be till I got to Emerald City.

As I was walking, I saw a farmer working out in his field plowing. I thought to myself how come he's using a horse and plow do they not know they have tractors nowadays? Maybe Oz is behind our time, but how can this be, if they have these types of coffee shops, maybe they are in both times in different parts of Oz. I will just have to do some research when I get home to find out what year mocha came into existence.

This part of Oz reminded me of the movie Song of the South.

Before I knew it, I was skipping along and singing the words to the song that Uncle Remus sings. Zippity doo- dah,-Zippity ay my oh my, what a wonderful day. That song is very true, yet it can be quite annoying. My little brother Frederick sings it repeatedly. Once he sings it about 3 times, it gets stuck in my head, and then I get really mad because it is an annoying song. Then my mom yells at me because I won't stop yelling at Frederick to shut up. That's a little snippet of my life. Sounds funny, huh?

Not really! I kept walking for a while until I came to a tiny village. As I was walking, I kept seeing people with suspenders, dorky glasses, and demented looks on their faces.

They all looked like Larry. He would fit right in. He is always wearing suspenders, and dorky glasses, and he always has a demented look on his face. Like he's constipated or something. But that isn't it. That was just the men and boys. Now try to think of what women and girls look like. They look like my sister Josie, with curly hair, and also dorky glasses. My life just gets crazy every minute. As I was thinking, a boy walked by and he weirdly looked like Larry. I thought *that can't be Larry. He is back in Lebanon.* Man, my life is just weird. I kept walking. I was not paying attention and I bumped into this tall, not dorky-looking teenager. He must not be from around here. He was hot! "Hiya, partner." I was so nervous that was all I could say.

"Hello." He answered. He had this amazing British accent. "You're not from around here, are you?" I asked him.

"No, I am not. And neither are you, by the looks of it," he said

"No, I'm not. How did you get here?"

"Well, it is a funny story. It all started when I was sitting in church, listening to the afternoon mass. I was quite mistakenly sitting in the queen's pew. I got caught and taken to the chief priest and suddenly I just disappeared and ended up in a little town called Pigment Land." He shuddered and continued, "Man, was that a weird town. Little pig-people running all around."

"Wait, I know that place. My brother Larry came to Oz before me and he landed in that place. He told us all about it. He thought it was kinda cool." I interrupted.

"Yeah, I guess it could be cool if you get past the point that they all talk. That is just creepy to me, not normal." Anyway, I started walking, and I just kept walking until I came to this little town. Say, do you know how to get back to the place that we both came from?"

"No, I don't but maybe we could ask someone where Emerald City is."

"Yeah, that could work. Let's go." They walked on.

"Hey, I didn't catch your name," I said.

"Zain." He answered.

"Oh, mine is Abigail."

" A very nice name, might I say." He replied. That made me blush so I just walked into my head down.

So on they went just jabbering as they kept a steady pace.

Zain was happy to have someone to walk with him. He was lonely being by himself.

"I have a sister that is 14, and she is a model and does some acting on stage. She was in the play Annie and she played Molly when she was 7."

I didn't have that great of adventure in life. To me, it seemed mostly like farm work and doing schoolwork.

"So what do you do when you are back home?" Zain asked.

"Not much I live on a farm. I have lots of chores to do and I'm homeschooled. I go to church and have gone to summer camp twice, but my life is boring. So how about you?"

"Well, I go to an all-boys military school. I'm in the chess club at school. I love to read mystery and Sci-Fi and also military stories. How about you, do you like to read?"

"Of course I do. I enjoy reading horse stories and Ann of Green Gables and lots of other stories."

Zain was happy they had something in common that they would enjoy talking about.

"Military people are cool. Even if they are just boys that are learning basic military skills." Zain said blankly.

"Sometimes I wish that my family didn't send me to military school. They are strict and I barely ever get to see my family because of it being a boarding school. That part of it is not very exceptional." He frowned.

Poor thing, I kinda felt pretty bad for him. Me being homeschooled means that I always get to see my family. Anyway, we may be together here till we get to Emerald City

Chapter 5

Zain looked over at me, "Do you know of a faster way to get to Emerald City?" he asked.

"If I did, wouldn't I be going that way? I have never been here before." I told him.

Turning to look at me, Zain replied, "You don't have to get so huffy about it!"

For some time, nobody said a word. It was so quiet all you could hear were the birds chirping and the stream moving. We glared at each other. Finally deciding to break the silence, I replied, "Well, sorry. It's kinda hard to find an easier way when I have never been here before."

I lowered my voice to control myself. "If I knew an easier way, I would most definitely tell you. And if I find a way, I will tell you right away because I know you want to get back to your family or school or whatever you're going to do, OK."

Zain just smiled and asked, "How old are you?

I replied, "13. How old are you?"

"I'm 15, but big for my age. You sure don't look 13 and you act older than your age. I thought you were 16."

I blushed and could not get a word out. I never had a guy I liked so much, but this could never be because after I get home, I will never see him again. My heart was heavy, and I was about to cry but did not want him to see me.

We were both getting thirsty, and we knew the stream could not be that far away because we could hear it.

We were almost there when I hear a scream. We both started running as fast as we could but to our surprise, all we saw was a boy pulling on a pineapple tree and the tree screaming. I couldn't believe that you could hear a pineapple tree scream. We just stood there watching. Then I understood why the tree was screaming.

With a mean look, the tree said, "The pineapples are still not ripe yet. It hurts when someone pulls on an unripe pineapple."

Zane's mouth was wide open in shock. I turned to look at him when I said "My brother Larry saw apple trees that talked."

Zain could not believe all this. It was new to him. Just like it was new to me.

Time was slipping by. The sun was setting, and we needed to find a place to sleep.

Zain saw a haystack and asked. "Why don't we sleep on the hay so that it would make a nice soft bed?

So that was the plan for the night. He was sure a gentleman. He slept on the side by the yellow brick road as I slept on the other side. It was sure a warm night, but I couldn't fall asleep because Zain was snoring so loudly. I was watching the stars and planets in the sky.

The next morning we both were very thirsty and the first thing we both said was: "We need to find that stream so we can get a drink."

We could hear the rushing sound of the stream. We headed in that direction. When we got here, we ran to the stream and knelt and kept drinking until we were so full of water we had to lie on our back and wait.

By that time it was noon and we had to make up for the lost time, and we hadn't even eaten breakfast or lunch yet.

Zain asked, "Do you think we can find food way out here?"

With a giggle "Maybe."

Zain replied, "We should set a rabbit trap."

I couldn't believe Zain would say this when we have no rope and box to trap a rabbit with.

Just then, up ahead, was a rope and box to trap a rabbit with. Zain was happy to see this. He looked at me and said; "I guess this will do."

I told Zain, "We can't just take someone else's trap and use it without the person giving us the okay."

But when we got to the trap, there was already a rabbit trapped. We both looked at each other, but I still opposed the idea.

"We can't eat someone else's meal. This might be for a poor family. Besides, it's stealing."

Zain took a big huff, and I could tell he was mad at me for not wanting to do this. If I don't do this, I might walk by myself and will have nobody to talk to.

It was a hard decision, but I gave in anyway and told Zain, "If you can kill the rabbit and skin it, then we can have dinner."

With a look of gratitude, he said, "I'm glad you changed your mind."

I just smiled as he pulled out his pocket knife and started working on our dinner.

Zain asked me to go get some wood for the fire as he skinned the rabbit. I wasn't sure where to look for wood but I just looked around and suddenly I spotted lots of twigs. I came back with an armload, but Zain said. "We need more twigs."

So off I went to get more. When I came back, the fire was going, and the meat was cooking.

It smelled so good and had the smell of onion. I asked Zain, "How can a rabbit smell like onions."

"I found some wild onions by the big oak tree behind you and rubbed the rabbit down with it and stuck the onions in the mouth."

We just sat on the giant boulder waiting for the meat to get done and we talked about the unique books we had read.

Eventually,y the meat was done and Zain took the meat off of the twig and placed it on the boulder. He looked around to find a rock to set the twigs on.

We started pulling the meat off the bones. We ate and ate until we were stuffed full. We finished every bite. I yawned, and that made Zain do the same thing. We both found a nice patch of grass close to the fire. We slept on opposite sides of the fire.

Chapter 6

Morning came before I knew it. It felt like I had just gone to sleep. Looking over at Zain, I saw that he was still sleeping. I didn't want to wake him, so I turned over and went back to sleep.

The next thing I knew, I heard noises coming from down the road. Looking over at Zain again I saw that he was still asleep. He sure is a late sleeper. I'm just going to wake him up, or otherwise, it's going to take us forever to get to Emerald City. I walked over to Zain and woke him up.

"What's happening? Why did you wake me up?"

"Nothing much I just woke you up because I can't leave you here by yourself. That's not safe. I wanted to see what all the commotion down the road was. It woke me up." I answered. This guy sure was inquisitive.

"Oh, that makes sense. Let's go." We started packing up the stuff that we didn't have. Meaning we didn't pack up at all. We had nothing to pack up. We started making our way to the road. Zain asked, "What do you think is going on?"

"I am not sure, but we are going to find out pretty soon. There it is right ahead. Look." I pointed.

He turned away from me and saw what I had previously seen. A marketplace like where my mom used to do farmers' markets. "Shall we go take a look?" Zain asked me.

"Sure why not!" I answered. "This marketplace is much bigger than where my mom sells her goat's milk soap bars. She could make more money from her soap here. She made quite a bit from selling at the farmers market in my hometown. Everyone likes her soap, saying it works miracles. I don't specifically like it; it dries out my hair." I was just blabbing again. Zain verified that theory.

"Just shut up and look at all this cool stuff." He turned to look at me. He smirked and said, "What a dork." We came up to a booth that, like Mom, sold soap. Now that is just plain creepy. Zain decided he was hungry, so we walked away and tried to find a place to eat. We decided that since we couldn't find a place to eat, we should ask someone for directions. We saw a man that looked like he was of some authority. "Sir, do you know where we could find some food around here?"

"Yes, I do. Lucky for you, you came here just in time for lunch. Follow me." We concluded that this man was someone that we could trust. "OK let's go." I said to Zain."I thought that you were hungry." He was being a slowpoke.

We started following him to wherever the lunch stuff was. When we came up to the table, we stopped dead in our tracks. There was so much food! I think Zain just about had a heart attack. We grabbed some plates and started getting food on our plates. We found a table and sat down to eat. It was the teenager's table because there were a whole bunch of teenagers that were sitting there eating. I'm kinda thinking that the girls like Zain because they kept staring at him, whispering and giggling. I was kinda hoping that he didn't like any of those girls. I had just barely thought that when a girl about 14 years old came up to Zain and struck up a conversation with him. Turns out that Zain wasn't the only one that was being looked at. A guy about 16 came up to me and started talking to me. "So you and your brother aren't from around here, are you?" He asked.

"No, we are not." I answered, "How can you tell?", I asked him. Zain looked at me with a funny look that made me laugh. Zain looked at the teenager and said "We are not siblings. We met awhile back and both decided to walk to Emerald City together, so we could see if the Wizard of Oz can help us get back home."

All at once, the teenagers were laughing at him. Even I looked at him strangely because I knew The Wizard was not there anymore.

A girl at the end of the table replied. "This shows you are not from around here, or you would have known that the Wizard left in a hot-air balloon many years ago and has not come back yet. He left the Tin Man, Scarecrow, and The Lion in charge until the day he returns.

The smallest teenager said. "Can you tell us how you came to Oz?"

Zain looked at me first, "You can start first."

I told them how I came to Oz and how I felt about being here.

After I was done, Zain spoke up and told me how he came to Oz.

The freckled face girl looked at Zain and said. "That was stupid of you to do. If anybody ever sat in the Wizard's chair we would go to jail for life."

I looked at Zain, and he looked at me, and we struggled to believe this.

We just finished eating when a cart came up to the table with so many desserts to pick from. My mouth was watering. Zain's eyes were popping out of his head.

The server asked me, "What 3 desserts would you like?"

I replied. "Dark Chocolate cake, Apple Betty, and, Pistachio Pudding."

She asked Zain what he would like "Strawberry cake, chocolate cake, and white chocolate cookies.", Zain replied.

After we ate we both said our goodbyes and once again we were on our journey.

Chapter 7

It was a never-ending journey, we both thought. It *seems like we will get nowhere.* It was a different type of place, with all kinds of interesting things in different cities. But despite that, we were tired of waking and walking and seeming to get nowhere.

Well, I wonder what would be around the corner next. You never know in Oz.

You could tell Zain was getting tired and just wanted to go home. He had just about enough of this place. But I liked every new place I saw. I was even thinking when I got home I could write a book about all my adventures.

As we neared the next town, we could both smell some chemicals but we could not tell what the smell was. The

chemical was making our noses itch. Zain was sneezing.

We came upon a sign that said Cosmetology University. It was a stunning place with a tall brick building and Japanese Cherry Blossom trees. Planted around the trees were crocus flowers of different colors.

There were benches under some trees. The grass was the brightest green I ever saw. On the lawn, there was a fountain that that it's spout looked like a giant hair dryer with water pouring out of it. It was quite interesting actually.

We both walked over to the fountain and got a closer look at it. Fantail guppies were swimming around.

Maybe I can ask Mom if we can have a fountain with fantail guppies. Then I remembered I lived on a farm that had ducks and geese. They would eat them and be swimming in the water. That's not good.

Maybe someday I can have one in front of my home, wouldn't that be nice?

"You know Zain, for the last two years I have been wanting to be a cosmetologist after I graduate from high school, and now I'm thinking, why can't I go to school here?"

"Are you joshing me?"

"No, why do you think I am?"

"Because if you go to school here and graduate, how are you going to get a job back home? People all think The Wizard of Oz is a fairy tale. Didn't you always think about this too?"

"I always did until my brother and sister went to Oz. Now I know it's a true place."

"If you are so interested in going to school here why don't you go get some information about this school."

"And how am I supposed to carry the information? Do you see me carrying a purse or wearing a backpack?."

"I'm just making a statement, don't get so huffy about this!"

"Sorry!"

"Well, we better keep walking so we can get there."

Coming in front of us was a Tandem bike. "I have never seen one of these types of bikes before in person, only in the movies."

"In my country, lots of people ride Tandem bikes."

Riding the bike were two little people in blue. Zain just looked at them funny.

As they rode on by they waved and said "Hi"

Zain and I replied. "Hi"

"By reading the books you should have known these were Munchkins," I said kind of accusingly.

"I never read the books before, or seen the movie."

"I thought most people would have at least read the book. Now that I think of it, it's kind of pathetic that you haven't even read any of the books or watched the movie. You need to do that someday, Okay?"

" Whatever you say," Zain said sarcastically.

We decided that since we didn't have a bag to put the info in, we might as well keep walking. As we were walking away we saw a table by the entrance that a college student was setting up.

"It's probably a table that is selling something and you know we do not have any money," Zain said sternly.

"Wel,l can't we just go take a look and see? Please? With sugar on top?" I stuck my bottom lip out like my little brother Frederick does when he wanted something.

"Okay. Okay, I guess we can just take a look. And then we are going to be on our way. Got it?"

"Yes. Now let's go check it out." We started to casually walk towards the table. I think Zain probably had a tiny little crush on the girl because he kept staring at her with stars in his eyes. Or maybe she reminded him of someone he knew and he was about to cry. The poor thing. I felt bad for him.

"Hello, how are you doing on this fine day?" the lady asked.

"We are doing good, and how are you?"

"Well, I am doing good. Would you like a brochure or anything," she asked us.

"You know what we would like a brochure if you have a bag to put it in."

"I have one left." she places the brochure in a canvas bag. The bag even had the name of the college embroidered on the front.

"Before you leave, next week we are having an open house on Tuesday at 4:00 if you like to come."

I didn't want to hurt her feelings so I said "I'll think about it."

Zain just gave me a strange look and I knew what he meant.

After we walked away Zain said, "You know we will not be able to come to the open house. Why did you lie?"

"I didn't lie. I said I was going to think about it and I will. I'll think about how it would not work out to go to school here."

Not much was said for a while.

Chapter 8

I was getting hungry, and I bet Zain was too. Over yonder, there was a cornfield, and in the ditch were lots of corn on the cob.

I ran over to the ditch and started picking them up. Zain walked over to me and said, "Are we allowed to do this?"

"I don't see why not. The ditch is not part of a farmer's land; it belongs to the city." We filled my bag up and being a kind young man he said, "I'll carry the bag."

We both kept looking for a spot where we could have dinner. Zain noticed up ahead that there was smoking coming over the hill.

"Let's go see where the smoke is coming from. Maybe we can cook the corn there."

I was getting tired. I needed to sit down. I just sat on the edge of the road.

"What are you doing?" Zain asked

"I'm too tired to go on"

"We must if you want to eat and find a place to sleep." That got me going. I was excited to find a place where I could sleep in a bed. If possible.

We made it to the top of the hill when we saw where the smoke was coming from.

It was plain Indians living in teepees like we have in America.

Zain just looked at me before saying a word "I have never seen them before where I live, we do not have them."

Zain just looked at me, with a funny look. That helped me to know that he did not understand a word of what I was saying.

"I thought the government stopped Indians from living in teepees as they did back in the 1800's"

"They did in the late 1800s. And actually, the government has gotten pretty lenient about the Indians and their reservations. They don't want to upset them so much that they would revolt. That would not be a very good thing. They do not want to make the same mistakes as the government in the 1800s. They are being smart." After I said all that I could tell that Zain was overwhelmed. So just to put his mind at rest I explained to him that I was a big history freak and that I knew a lot about different historical subjects.

"There would be days that I would just sit down and read history books. I had a series that I like called the Dear America series. It's all about the girls and their experiences during different times in history, like the Titanic and World War 2.Things like that." I paused to catch my breath. Zain was just sitting there listening to every word that I said.

"If I don't want to be a cosmetologist I could be a history teacher because I know so much," I asked Zain, " What do you think?"

Zain looked at me with this weird look and said, "Well, you know what, you could be anything that you wanted to be and you would be just the same Abbie that I know now. Still amazing, still funny, and still the motormouth that I know now." At the last statement, he smirked.

"You know Zain, you can be an annoying person. But you know what, I can be an annoying person at times, so yeah. Anyway, you can ask my mom and she will tell you that I am a very annoying child." I took a breath after all that I had said.

Zain got a faraway look in his eyes. Probably thinking of his mom and dad.

Chapter 9

We started walking again and talked about pretty much nothing. We decided that we would go down to the Indian village and ask them if we could eat some food. We made our way toward the village. When we got close to the village we saw a group of kids playing in the dirt. We went up to the kids and asked, "Can we use your campfire to cook our corn?" They were happy to have visitors and they said yes. They grabbed our hands and took us to see the chief of the tribe and the chief, Chief Winter Wolf, brought us into his teepee and showered us with gifts and stuff. I don't know much about Indian festivities but I do know that this was not a normal thing that they did. I went to one of the kids and asked her, "Why are they giving us all of these gifts?" I was honestly very confused.

The little girl laughed and said, "Well this is a wedding celebration for you and your man.

Well, that was not what I was expecting to hear, so I asked. "Who told you that we were getting married?"

"Your man told us." She smiled. I pointed to Zain and asked, "Him?"

She smiled again, "Yes him." OK, that was the end of these shenanigans. I walked up to Zain and asked, "Zain, why did you tell them that we were getting married?"I was steaming mad at this point.

He smiled. "Well, I was just trying to see how you would react. And anyway,y they already said that we were a cute couple. I just agreed to that and I just needed a way to tell you."

He seemed sorry now. "It was just supposed to be a joke. Sorry." He looked down and would not make eye contact.

"Zain, that was not funny. At all. Come on, let's go. We need to get to Oz as quickly as we can. Then I can go home and get away from you. Ughhh!!!" I was infuriated. I kinda felt bad. We said goodbye and started walking out of the village. With every step I took, I felt even worse. After about an hour I couldn't take it anymore. I just had to apologize for overreacting. I walked over to Zain who had stopped to take a break after walking nonstop for an hour.

"Zain?"

"What!"

At least he was talking to me. "I need to talk to you, Will you talk to me?"

"Sure."

"Well I just wanted to apologize for overreacting back at the Indian village and I just wanted to say sorry. Will you forgive me for blowing up at you ?" He turned to me and tried to smile but it came out as a grimace.

"It's ok. I shouldn't have done that to you anyway. It was mean and I wasn't thinking of your feelings." Now he smiled.

I couldn't resist his gorgeous smile so I said, "That's ok." I stuck out my hand for him to shake. Instead, he pulled me into a big bear hug. It was kinda awkward but also amazing. It felt good to be hugged. After he let me go we started to walk again. I had a feeling that this was going to be a long journey that we were going on together. It might be fun but it might be stressful who knows? We were walking for a while when all of a sudden Zain took my hand and we started walking hand in hand. And you know what, I didn't even mind at all. We were walking and walking and all that we saw was a bunch of fields and stuff. A bunch of corn, grass, and more corn. "You know what, when I get home I am not going to want to eat any corn after all of this stupid corn. Ughhh, just go away you stupid corn!!!!!!!!" Zain yelled.

Chapter 10

We finally came up to a little town and we saw that the sun was starting to set so we decided that we should ask someone if we could stay at their house for the night. We walked down the street and came up to a little shop and we saw a lady that looked like a good candidate for asking if we could stay at their house for the night. We went into the little shop and went up to the lady and said to her,

"Hello ma'am, we just have a question to ask you. Do you mind?"

She turned to us and said, "Sure, go ahead."

"Thank you. We were wondering if maybe we could stay at your house for the night. We just need a place to stay and then we are going to be on our way. We promise." Zain said.

The lady gave us a very suspicious look and said, "Well why do you need a place to stay? You should be at home with your parents."

Zain and I looked at each other and we decided that we should just wing it. At least that's what I got from our little eye conversation so I answered by saying, " Well we both ran away and we decided that we should go home and talk it out with our parents and so that is why we need a place to stay."

She just stood there staring at us and it seemed like a lifetime she was looking at us, she finally broke down and said "Okay!"

After she locked the place up she said " Come back with me." She showed us the steps and said "My home is above the shop."

When we got upstairs it was a quaint little place with the smallest kitchen I have ever seen and a small living room, I asked the lady, " Where do you sleep?"

"I have a Murphy bed. I have two mats you can put down on the floor to sleep on. They are behind the couch."

Zain went and got them and placed them both by the open window.

"I have some stew on the back burner, it's not much but I would be willing to share with you."

We both thanked her and sat at the little table that was part of the kitchen.

She placed the bowls in front of us along with a loaf of homemade bread. The stew smelled so good. She placed two glasses half full of red wine by the bowls. We did not want to hurt her feelings so we just thanked her and drank it. We were not used to wine, at all.

After dinner, the lady asked us, "Would you like to play Rummy."

Zain and I just looked at each other with a bit of confusion. Zain said, " I don't believe I have ever played rummy before. Have you Abigail?"

I haven't so I told the lady, "I think I would like to play rummy with you I'd you wouldn't mind teaching me."

She explained how to play it, and it was lots of fun. Before we knew we were playing for a couple of hours.

"I think it's time we all got to bed." Said the lady.

We did as we were told. We headed to our mats and laid down to head to the land of nod. Before long we were all fast asleep. Well except for me. I could not fall asleep with two people snoring. I found a small pillow and covered one ear up and the other was on the mat but it still did no good. I could hear them.

Morning came before too long and I was just falling asleep when Zain woke me up.

I just lay there for a minute and stretched out. When I got up I placed the mat behind the couch and walked to the table where Zain was sitting.

Just as I was sitting down, the lady placed a bowl of porridge with raisins on top of it and a glass of apple juice in front of us both.

She looked at us both and in a soft voice said, "You need a healthy filling breakfast to start your day with. I hope you get back home safe."

We looked at each other and said, "We will."

We said our goodbyes and off we went not knowing what lay ahead.

We found that it was a very pretty little town and it would be ok to stay a while and look around at all the sights that there were to see. There were so many it was almost overwhelming. Imagine it, you're walking along and keep finding all of these wonderfully awesome things that you wish you could buy but don't have any money. Imagine that you are walking in a mall and you see all of these wonderful shoes and you're all like "OMG! I can't even believe that these are so stinking gorgeous I just wish that I could buy them!", Then you keep walking along and you keep finding pretty prom dresses. (if you are a girl of course.) I have nothing against boys at all. The only problem is that I am a girl and I can relate to girls even better than I can boys and why are boys even reading a book about a hairdresser?

Oh and don't tell me that you boys are now starting to wear prom dresses! And you are all like, OMG! That is just the most amazing thing ever. I wish that I could go and get that and wear it to the prom. If you go to the prom of course. I mean hey, maybe you are homeschooled. Don't judge what happens to people.

Chapter 11

Zain was getting mad because it seemed like we were getting nowhere "Ain't we ever going to get to Oz? It seems like I have been here for 5 years and it has only been about a month!"

"It can't be that far-off or could it?" I asked.

"I wouldn't know, I haven't been here before."

I noticed not far off there was a well, " Do you see what I see up ahead? I asked.

"Sure do."

"I'll race you there," I said.

I was so far ahead of Zain that it seemed like he was running in slow motion.

I just stood there waiting for the slowpoke to get there whenever he decided to mosey on this way.

"You're a fast runner for a girl."

With my hand on my hips and a look that could kill,l I said, "What is that supposed to mean!"

"It was just a statement that you are a fast runner for a girl."

"You mean a girl can't run faster than a boy."

" Never mind." He just looked dejected.

As I turned around I noticed a sign that said this is a wishing well not meant for drinking.

"I wish I had a penny to throw in the wishing well," I said.

Zain saw something shiny on the ground bending over. He picked it up. It was just what he needed. It looked like a penny but it had the Oz logo on both sides.

"This must be Oz type of penny," I said.

He handed it to me, "You can make a wish."

"You found it, you make a wish." I handed it back to Zain.

He closed his eyes and without saying a word he made his wish. I didn't know it at the time but he wished that we could get out of Oz right at that moment.

We had just turned away from the well when we heard a noise coming from it. We turned back toward it and looked over the edge. All we could see was something green coming up the well.

Zain grabbed my arm and pulled me away from the well. We were no more than 2 feet away when the bubble engulfed us both.

Sending us high up in the sky. We both were scared. We had no clue where they were heading.

It seemed like forever before we saw anything. In the distance, we saw bright green lights shining up toward the sky.

I was so happy I kept yelling "We must be heading to the Emerald City!"

"Are you sure?" Zain didn't seem so sure.

"I keep forgetting you've never read any of the Oz series." I tried to explain a little bit about some of the series to give him some context on why I thought that we were on our way to Emerald City.

As we got closer we could see lots of people outside of Emerald City looking up at us and pointing to the sky.

The bubble slowly went down and it landed on the grass in front of all the people.

We just sat inside the bubble for what seemed like forever. Slowly the little people came closer. Before long, they parted to make a path. Coming down the path were Cowardly, Scarecrow, and the Cowardly Lion. Following close behind them were Dorothy and the Toto.

As they stood in front of us the bubble magically disappeared.

Chapter 12

We just stood there for a moment taking this all in. Before long the Scarecrow spoke up, "Nice to meet you both."

"Likewise." We both replied simultaneously.

I was the first one to talk directly ly to the Scarecrow. "Hi I'm Abigail and this is Zain."

The Scarecrow just stared at me with a look like he had seen me before but couldn't place who I was.

"You've been here before?" asked the Scarecrow.

"I haven't but my brother, Larry, has."

"Oh yes, I remember him, how is he doing?"

"Okay, I guess. I haven't been home." I chuckled.

"Would you like to come inside and see the Emerald City?, asked the Scarecrow.

"Sure," we both replied

We both followed behind the Scarecrow, Tin Man, Cowardly Lion, and Dorthy. Last, but not least, was Toto.

As the double green doors opened, I noticed that almost everything was some shade of green. Except for the horse. It turned different colors.

I also noticed that to my left there was a beauty shop. Upon seeing this I thought to myself, *Man that sure would be a nice place to work. Maybe I could work there, never know unless I ask.*

If this wasn't the prettiest place I had ever seen in my life I don't know what it was.

We all walked over to the fountain and sat on the edge. I turned my head to look into the fountain. It was the bluest water I had ever seen. There were all kinds of fish in there in assorted colors. It looked like a fishy rainbow.

The Lion scratched his neck and then turned to look at me "Tell us how you came to Oz?" He told me.

"Well you see, my sisters and I were doing our hair and I got a butterfly barrette stuck in my hair. My sisters both tried to get it out but had no luck. The next thing I knew the butterfly barrette was pulling me up in the air. After that, before I knew it, I was landing in Oz."

"Well, Zain, tell us how you got here?" said Tinman.

"I was going to the Catholic church and I walked up to the front pew and sat where the queen and her family always sat. The next thing I knew the priest took me to his office. All I remember after this is being in a town here in Oz called Pigment Land."

The Scarecrow just sat there looking at Zain and me for a moment. "Well, how can we help you both?" he finally asked.

Zani took a deep breath before speaking. " I would just like to go home if that's okay with you."

"I think I can arrange that." Without saying another word the Scarecrow walked away.

The Scarecrow went to his ring safe and grabbed a ring. Just before he shut the safe he thought that he might as well get a ring for Abigail just in case she would want to go home as well.

In a matter of minutes, the Scarecrow was back and handed Zain a ring. Zain just stared at it for a moment then asked. "What is this ring for?"

"Would you be so kind as to stand up, please?"

Zain stood to his feet looking the Scarecrow in the eyes.

"Now take the ring and place it on your left fourth finger and when you want to go home twist the ring twice and say please send me back home. If you ever want to come back to visit Oz just twist the ring twice and say send me back to Emerald City."

The Scarecrow did the same thing to me. "Is there anything else you want to say before going back home?

"I was wondering if I could come back and go to college in Oz. I want to be a cosmetologist and would love to live in Brewerville."

"Why here?" The Scarecrow asked.

"It's sure a lovely place so colorful and most of the people are friendly. It makes you feel at peace. It's not like where I come from there is so much hate in the world and killing Plus, I love the smell of coffee." I explained to the Scarecrow.

" Let me talk it over with the Tinman and the Cowardly Lion first before making up my mind. Why don't you both go over and get some cotton candy to eat and look around." the Scarecrow pulled two tokens out of his pocket for each of them, "This will cover the cost of the cotton candy."

After we got our cotton candy, I looked at Zain and said "Wouldn't you love to live in Emerald City or another part of Oz?"

"I never gave it much thought. But it sure is a pretty place, but much different than where I come from."

"I can understand what you mean," I replied.

It seemed like we were walking around Emerald City. In reality, we were walking around for like an hour and then all of a sudden all the leaders of Oz came up behind us and kinda startled us.

The Scarecrow looked at us and said, " We made up our minds. Abigail, you can come back and go to college and work in the beauty shop in Emerald City. You'll come back and live in an apartment on the outskirts of the city. Everything g will be paid for. Your food, rent, everything. All until you arc done with college." He explained. I was in awe of what he said. "One more thing. Your parents and family can not come and see you unless they have the okay from us. Most likely your parents will not but I will give them a special mirror that can never be broken and they can see you and talk to you just like you can talk on a phone. In that way, you will be able to keep in contact with your family."

The Cowardly Lion looked at me and asked. "How old are you?"

"I'm 13 years old."

"Well, you have to finish school where you live and then you come back." I was so happy I gave each of them a hug and thanked them all.

"Zain you can come back anytime after you have been home for three weeks in your time." Tin Man Said

Zain thanked them all with a handshake.

"Are you both ready to go home?" Asked the Scarecrow.

"I guess so," I replied.

"How about you, Zain?" He asked.

"Ready, but can I say one thing?

"Sure", said the Scarecrow.

Zain took my hand and looked me in the eye. "I have never met anybody like you but when you get older I want to marry you. I know we won't be able to see each other very often but I know that some say I will see you again. Is there any chance I could get your address?"

" Wait. Hold up. You want to marry me? Oh.... Yes, you may have my address. I would love to write back and forth with you." I was flabbergasted. I was only 13 and I already had been practically proposed to. I reached into the bag that the girl at the college gave me and going a piece of paper and a pen. I wrote down my address and tore the piece of paper in half so that Zain could write down his address. He did and then he told me, " Now twist your ring and let's go back home."

Before long we were back home at the same spot that we were when we left to go to Oz.

Chapter 13

I looked around the bathroom and noticed that my two sisters were still in the bathroom. I smiled at them and said, "Hey guys, I'm back!!"

My sisters looked at me like I was crazy. Blair looked at me and said, " Abby, you didn't even go anywhere. How could you be back if you never left?" She looked at me like I was just a pathetic little kid that didn't know a thing.

"Yes, I have. I went to Oz." I told them.

They both looked at each other and said, "Whatever Abigail."

I rolled my eyes and showed them my ring. " Ok then since you don't believe me, how do you explain this ring with the Oz logo on it? And what about this bag that came from the beauty school in Oz? Hmm, how do you explain that!" I showed them my college bag and then I just looked at them like THEY were the ones that didn't know a thing.

I could tell they believed me then because their eyes lit up and Blair said, " Of I almost forgot, Larry went to Oz like last year or something like that. When he got back it was like nothing ever happened. Sorry, Abigail, I thought for sure you were crazy." Blair looked at me apologetically.

Josie turned to me with a sweet smile, "And don't forget, I was there too. Welcome back."

"Let's go to the living room and you can tell us all about what happened. " Blair suggested.

When we got to the living room Darla, Frederick, and Larry were sitting there, and when they saw us they asked, "What are you guys doing?"

", Oh hush would you. Abigail went to Oz and she's going to tell us all about it. If you can't be quiet go to your bedroom and leave us alone to listen. " Blair said strongly.

My parents, Jake and Connie, along with Albert walked into the house through the back door and heard the last part of what Blair had said.

"What's all the excitement?" Mom asked.

Darla yelled, way too loudly I might add, "ABIGAIL WENT TO OZ JUST LIKE LARRY AND JOSIE!!!"

"Oh no, here we go again Dad said. They all sat down and started to listen as I told the story of all that had happened. From the barrette to meeting Zain to Brewerville and everything else. I told them how the Scarecrow, Tin Man, Lion, and Dorothy told me that I could go back and go to college. I also told them about how Zain said he was goto ing marry me.

"Now you hear me, Abigail. I'm just going to say this once. You are not getting married unless I meet the guy and that will be a very long time. Plus you might meet someone else along the way. You are only 13, you know." My dad said.

My mom looked at my dad like he was crazy but I caught him winking at her. I could tell they didn't believe the whole story and my dad only said those things to cater to my "imagination". Parents sometimes...

The weeks went into months and all I could think of was Oz and Zain and the possibility of living there in Oz with Zain. I worked hard on all of my homework so that I could get done with high school and I did all of my chores well and I even asked my parents if they needed anything done around the farm. I was keeping busy because it kept my brain from wandering and thinking about Zain.

After a while, I decided to start preparing for when I went to my new home in Oz. I thought I should make some pretty things to kind of decorate so I started making bowl cozies to use with my bowls. I made enough that I could sell them at the shop my mom owned so that she wouldn't notice that I was making so many. I also didn't want her to catch on to the fact that I was making them to take to Oz.

Chapter 14

After Zain got back home from Oz, his parents had a surprise for him.

"We decided not to have you stay in the dorm anymore. You will come home after school and live here. We miss you too much, we just don't want to see you only in the summer." Mum said

Zain was so happy he gave them both a hug and thanked them.

Zain was studying hard in school and started reading all the Wizard of Oz books in the series and other Oz books. He was even watching the Wizard of Oz movie and any other type of Oz movie. Even cartoon versions. Today he was thinking he should buy all of the Wizard of Oz books and the movies and everything so that one day when he had kids, they could all enjoy watching it and seeing what a wonderful place Oz was.

What joy he had in doing this, but every day he still thought of Abigail and could not wait until they were married. One day as he was sitting at home reading a book when he started wondering why Abigail had not written to him yet.

A knock on his door cleared his mind for a second. Opening his door he found his sister standing there. "Papa told me to come to tell you supper is ready. " She said.

"Can I ask you a question?" Zain asked her.

"Sure" she answered.

"If you give a girl your address so she could write to you and it has been more than a year and she has not yet written does it mean she has forgotten about you?"

"Sometimes it does but other times some girls think the guy should make the first move. That is just how they have been raised. So I would say after dinner get busy and write her a letter and maybe send her a picture of you to remind her of you."

"Thanks, sis."

Zain's dad stood at the bottom of the steps and yelled up. "Are you two coming down to dinner?"

"Yes, Papa!" they both replied.

It seemed like dinner would never be over. Finally, his plate was empty and his mother brought a double chocolate carrot cake to the table.

He knew he couldn't leave the table until after dessert was over.

As he was eating, he thought, I *should get all of Mum's recipes and give them to Abigail.*

The next day Zain was up bright and early before going to school he put his mom's recipe cards in his backpack. At school in the library, they had a copy machine they could use for free. If they had an ASB card, you had to slide the card each time you used the copy machine.

It took Zain about 15 minutes to get every recipe copied and put in his locker before his friends showed up for school.

Just as he grabbed his math book out of his locker his best friend Philip came up with a smile on his face.

"What are you so happy about?" Asked Zain

"My dream has come true. Papa and Mum are taking our family on a trip to America and we are going to DisneyWorld in Florida this summer."

"Wow, that's great! Well, you'll never guess what happened last week when we were out of school for parent conferences. Have you ever read the Wizard of Oz book series?" Zain asked his friend.

"Some of it," replied Philip."

"Last Sunday when I went to church I wasn't thinking, and I sat in the Queen's spot."

Phillip looked surprised for a moment before he said, "Well, what happened?"

"The Priest saw I was sitting there and came down and grabbed my arm and took me into his office. The next thing I knew, I was somewhere in Oz."

"You must have dreamed this. Or you are just pulling my leg? You better not say this to anybody or they will laugh at you and call you crazy, and nobody will speak to you all year." Phillip.told Zain. And then he said under his breath a bit, "I guess I have to speak to you because we are best friends."

" Well don't believe me then! " Zain said strongly. Then he slammed his locker closed and walked off.

Chapter 15

There was a group of guys behind Phillip and one of them rapped him on the shoulder and asked him what had just happened. Phillip struggled to figure out if he should tell all of them about what Zain had said or if he shouldn't because Zain was his best friend. In the end, he decided that he shouldn't say anything so he just looked the guy in the eye and said, " I don't have the foggiest eye."

Zain could not wait until school was over so he could put his Mums recipe box back where it belonged before she knew it was missing.

Finally, the last bell of the day rang, and he jumped out of his seat, hurried to his locker, grabbed the recipe box, and put it in my backpack along with my homework.

He was hurrying down the hallway when Philp came by and tries to talk to me. "No time to talk now, got to go!" Phillip shrugged his shoulders.

As soon as Zain opened the door his mother yelled from the kitchen, "Is that you Zain?"

"Yes, Mum." *How am I going to get Mum's recipe box back in the kitchen before she knows it's gone,* he thought.

Just as he was thinking that the phone in the hallway rang, "I'll get it, Mum! " He yelled.

" Hello? " He said into the receiver.

"Hi, is your mum there?" It was one of his Mums friends.

"One second let me go get her. " He told the woman. "Mum! The phone's for you!"

Here's my chance to put the recipe box back where it goes. He thought. Right as he put the recipe box back where it went, his mother walked into the kitchen. To cover up what he was doing he reached into the cupboard to grab a glass and then he walked over to the sink to get a drink of water.

"Did you have a good day at school?" Mum asked

"I guess it was like any other school day." After finishing his water, he excused himself and then went upstairs to do his homework for the day. As he was doing his homework he thought, I *wish we had a phone upstairs that I could call Phillip on. I want to talk to him about the rest of what happened in Oz. I want to be able to tell him about Abigail. But he thought I was pulling his leg. Well, better get back to doing my history homework.*

All was quiet in the house for a long time and then the phone rang.

Zain's mum yelled from the bottom of the steps "Zain the phone is for you! It's Philip!"

After the day that Zain had at school, he now wondered what Phillip was calling about. He answered anyway, "Hello?"

"Hey, Zain I was just calling to say I'm sorry for not believing you when you were telling me about everything that went down at the church. I was wondering if you could tell me all that happened in Oz?" Phillip said.

"Not now, everyone around will hear me."

"Hear what?" asked his sister.

"You never mind!"

"Tomorrow after school, if you don't mind walking home with me, we can talk more about this?" Phillip wondered to Zain.

They both said goodbye and hung up the phone with a click.

The next day as they both were walking home Zain told Phillp everything that happened to him on his adventures in Oz.

"You think I can go with you sometimes?"

"I guess I could ask. Oh, I almost forgot to show you the ring." Zain exclaimed.

"Wow!!!!" Phillip was amazed at the ring.

"I'll see you tomorrow," Zain said.

"Same time, same place," Philip said.

As he opened the door to his house as he got there he yelled, "I'm home! Anyone here?"

"I'm upstairs in your room," his mum said.

When he got to his room his mum was changing the sheets. How he loved the fresh smell of sheets that hung on the clothesline outside and having his bed aired out all day.

This was one thing he hoped that Abigail would do when they got married.

He unzipped his backpack and took out his test paper and showed his mum. "Look, I got an A+ on my math test," Zain told his mom.

"I'm so proud of you I knew you could do this."

Mum kissed him on my forehead and turned to walk away but before she did she told Zain, "This calls for your favorite meal. Bacon meatloaf."

Just then Zain's father was heard walking through the door as he was coming home from work. Zain couldn't wait to tell his father about his aced math test. He ran downstairs and hugged his father before showing his father the test and saying, "I just got my math test back, and I got an A+!" He took the paper from Zain's hand and looked it over.

"I knew you had it in you, son. I'm very proud of you." He took out a five-dollar note. He never got money for good grades before this!

"Thank you!"

Chapter 16

I was outside working in the garden with Tammy and Larry when the Mail lady drove up to deliver the mail. Larry went to get it and brought it for Mom.

As my mom was looking through the mail, she noticed a letter addressed to me. She just looked at it for a while wondering what in the world she should do with it. This wondering was because it was from a boy, you see. So after a while, she decided to take it up with her husband so she went outside to get my dad from the roof where he was working and yelled up to him, " Jake! Get down here we need to talk!! Abby got a letter from a boy!"

Jake was so upset about the letter that he tripped over a hammer and started sliding off the roof.

We were all just standing there watching as he was falling off and then at lady second he grabbed the drainpipe and was holding on for dear life.

"Help get the ladder!" He yelled. Blair was the one that was the fastest at getting the ladder and she got it over to our dad just in time because as he was just getting onto the first rung of the ladder the drainpipe came off and fell to the ground. Without my dad, thankfully, because of the quick thinking Blair.

Mom yelled at the top of her lungs, "Abigail, you get over here now and explain this letter from England!!"

My heart was pounding a mile a minute. It was hard for me to breathe. I didn't know what would happen.

My hand was shaking when I took the letter from Mom. I slowly opened the letter, but before I did I glanced around at everyone.

Dear, Abigail

How have you been? I have not heard from you since you left Emerald City.

I thought you must have forgotten about me, but I never forgot about you.

Someone told me that lots of women do not make the first move when writing a letter, so I took it upon myself to do so.

You will never guess what happened when I got back home, Papa and Mum decided to have me live at home not live in the military dorms. But, I still go to Military School.

But it's great to be home every day with my family. My sister is still acting. She got a part in the stage play Wizard of Oz. She's playing Dorothy. It's kind of funny actually. When my sister got the part in the play, I had just started to read all of the books in the series and was studying up for the next time I go there.

I got around to watching the movie and the cartoon. Also the TV version, and I bought a coloring book of The Wizard of Oz and I'm collecting the books too. So when we do get married and have children they can read the books also.

Have you been back to Emerald City? I have not yet but I'm going to go soon.

Well, I better end this letter and get some sleep. I love you with all my heart. Hoping to hear from you soon.

Love, Zain Tomas

When I went to put the letter back in the envelope I noticed a book of stamps. I pulled it out and counted how many stamps there were. I could write Zain twenty letters.

My heart was leaping for joy.

"Can I write Zain back? Please?!?" Mom walked over to where Dad was standing I could not hear what they were saying but eventually Mom came back and looked me in the eye. "We decided you can write him back, but you must tell Zain that we said that you guys could only write as friends and pen pals nothing else. We will read your first letter to make sure that you are telling him that." She told me.

"I will!" But in the back of my mind, I was thinking that I didn't have to SEND the letter. I could write the one that my mom wants me to write and then I can just throw it away and then write another one that I want to write and sent THAT one.

"But we still have to punish you with no movies for the next two nights and you will do everybody else's chores."

"I didn't ask him to write to me, that's not fair!" I exclaimed.

"Do you want me to add two more days of their chores?"

"No!"

"Then don't talk to me that way again. I'm the parent and know what is best for you and you do not need a boyfriend right now. Put the letter up and start on night chores. Feed the cats first and then give them some milk for a treat."

I opened the front door and when I got inside; I slammed it shut.

I went into my bedroom and put the letter in my purse so I would not lose the letter and stamps.

When I came back out my Dad looked at me and said: "I never want you to slam the door again. For doing that you now have to pick up all of the hay bale strings."

I said nothing, I knew it was better not to. I just walked away to start on my chores.

Chapter 17

That night when my brothers and sisters were watching a movie, I decided I didn't want to watch the movie, so I sat up in my bunk bed and wrote a reply to the letter.

Dear Zain,

It was very nice to hear from you. I'm glad your parents are letting you live at home and not in the dorms.

It was a surprise to hear that you read and watched the Wizard of Oz movies

My two goats had kids last week and one had twins. The other one just had one.

I'm reading the book Brotherhood of Betrayal by Randall Arthur. So far I like the book. If you have not read the book yet I recommend it.

My cat Sunshine is pregnant; this would be her first litter.

I'm sewing bowl cozies to sell at my mother's shop. I also made my pajamas, I'm getting pretty good at sewing. My parents said I'm too young to be thinking of marriage so I can only write to you as a pen pal.

From your friend Abigail

I recopied the letter taking out the pen-pal and added:

I can't wait till we are married and can live in Oz and have children.

I hope I can bring my goats and cat with me to Oz. They are a joy to me.

Well, gotta go and read my Bible before going to bed, take care I miss you a lot.

Love Abigail

I jumped off my bed with the letter in my hand and walked into the kitchen. Mom was making dinner when I asked her if she would read the letter before I mailed it.

Mom took the letter and read it. "Now that's better and he will get the right idea that you are too young to be thinking of getting married," she told me.

I went back into my room and put the other letter in the envelope and licked it shut and placed a heart sticker on the back of the envelope and the stamp on the front.

That night I could not sleep because I had to wake up in time to get this letter in the mail.

Morning came and I took the letter outside and waited for the mail lady to finally show up and I handed her my letter and she gave us our mail.

I took the mail inside and laid it on the table, went back outside, and started on my chores. Dad was already awake and had a burn pile going. I walked over and picked up the empty dog food bag and put the other letter inside the bag and threw it into the fire.

Just then, Dad came up behind me. "Good morning"

I turned around and was scared that my dad saw what I did. If he did, he said nothing.

Chapter 18

After 4 weeks, I was getting worried that my letter never got to Zain. *How am I going to live without hearing from him?* That night, Mom and Dad left to go out to dinner with their friends the Smiths.

I was sitting on my bunk bed looking over at Tammy and asking if she would play, "How Do I Live Without You by Trisha Yearwood."

Tammy picked up her cell phone and went to YouTube to look up the song. At first, it didn't want to play. She tried it once more, and it said no internet. She turned off her cell phone, counted slowly to ten, and turned it back on. This time the song played.

As the song was playing, Josie and Blair walked into the bedroom, and gave me a look that looked like what the heck is playing."Go away!" I yelled.

"What is it with you?" Blair asked.

"Nobody understands how I feel. I'm truly in love with Zain and miss him daily. This isn't just puppy love. You'll see one day."

My sister just left the room and went into the living room to watch the movie. I sat on my bed and was crying until Blair yelled, "We are going to watch Tiger Cruise. Are you coming to watch it with us?"

"No! I'm going to read The Hobbit," I replied

Larry stood by my bedroom door and said, "Abigail, would you like to play UNO with me."

"I just said I was going to read. Are you deaf?"

"I have nothing to do, I'm bored."

"It's not my problem that you're bored."

Tammy looked over at Larry. "Go read a book or do a word search."

"I don't feel like it!" Larry said in a snotty voice and turned and walked away.

Larry opened the front door and slammed the door shut. The next thing we knew, he was riding his bike around the farm.

Tammy looked over at me and said, "At least Larry's not bugging you now."

"I guess you are right."

We both went back to reading, hoping nobody else would disturb us, but 5 minutes later Darla and Frederick showed up at our bedroom door, both saying, "We have nothing to do."

I sat up and told them to go outside and play with Larry.

They both said, "Do we have to?"

"Well no, you can both take a nap. Is that better?"

Darla looked at Fredrick. "I think we will go outside and play," she replied.

They both ran to the front door and opened it and slipped on their boots.

Blair yelled," Shut the door!

Darla ran back and slammed the door shut.

For a long time, everything was quiet.

Just then, the house phone rang. Josie ran to pick up the phone.

"Hi, Mom, what's up?"

" We'll be home in a bit with dinner. Make sure the little kids are in their pajamas, and also make sure Larry cleaned the bathroom. It's his turn. After he's done cleaning the bathroom. Then you guys can watch a movie." she told me

Josie told Larry what their mom told him to do, and then told the little kids to get pajamas on.

Abigail jumped off her bunk bed and walked into the living room. "Josie, did you forget to tell Mom that some of us watched a movie already!"

"Don't worry about it. Mom did not ask, so I'm not lying. Go back and read your book."

It took Larry longer than everyone thought it would to clean the bathroom. By the time he was finished, Mom had just walked in.

Before Mom had even shut the front door, she looked at us all, "Did you know there are 20 goats out running around and some were even on the road? No movie until you guys pick up all of the movies on the floor and all of the books as well. Then you guys can go out and put all of the goats away. When you're done, give each goat a scoop of grain and check their water. If it's only half full and fill the bucket again. Fredrick and Darla, go look for chicken eggs. Leave one in the nest and mark which one you leave with this marker. Now go!!" She started shooing us out the door and we all ran out.

We all rushed to get our boots from the porch and get to the jobs that Mom had out before us.

As I was out doing my chores, I heard a voice saying it was coming from the chicken coop. *Could it be the same chicken that talked to my brother Larry?* I thought.

Slowly I walked toward the coop until I was standing by the chicken that was looking at me. *Could this be the one that was talking?*

"Over here, I'm the one that was talking to you." I looked over and it was one of our reddish chickens looking up at me. It was the one that was talking. I had to stand there and take deep breaths to compose myself before I gave it my full attention. When I did it asked, "Remember how your brother got to Oz?"

"Yes", I answered.

"Well, did you know that you can go down the same hole as your brother and end up in the land of Pigment?

Apparently, it hadn't known I had already been to Oz because when I said, "I've already been to Oz", it just looked at me in disbelief.

"Let me tell you everything that happened in Oz." I grabbed one of the green water tubs and turned it over so that I could sit down on it.

I explain how I went to Oz with a butterfly barrette and all of my fun adventures. And how I fell in love with a handsome teenager and he even asked me to marry him. I stopped to get my breath, and the chicken thought I was done talking.

"So let me get this straight. You are going to marry a teenager from Oz?" It asked.

"No, he is not from Oz. He is British and from England." I could not believe I was standing here talking to a chicken. I mean come on people were going to think I was crazy. Just as I turned away, I remembered it can't be any different from when I was in Oz. Talking to animals, scarecrows, a Tin Man, oh, and don't forget the cowardly Lion.

I turned back around and walked back to the chicken coop to finish my conversation.

Larry was feeding the goats and he turned to look at me. He gave me a little smirk and then went back to feeding the animals.

Before long, my mom opened the sliding glass door and yelled at me.

"Abigail, why are you just sitting on the bucket? There are lots of chores that need to be done. Now get to it!!"

Chapter 19

Back in England, Zain was over at Phillip's. They were watching The Wizard of Oz. It was Phillip's first time watching the movie, and it was Zain's 4th time watching the movie. Just as the flying monkeys appeared, Phillip bolted off the couch and fell on the hardwood floor with a thump.

The next thing Zain knew, he was laughing so hard he fell off the couch onto the floor as well.

For the rest of the movie, they just leaned up against the couch on the floor watching the movie.

Phillip's mum came into the living room and told Zain, "You might want to head home because it is starting to rain and you don't want to get all wet. Plus it's getting dark and I don't want your mom to be worrying about you."

"Yes, Ma'am" Zain replied.

He said his goodbyes and was home before the rain came down too hard.

Zain's mum heard the door slam shut. "Zain, is that you?"

"Yes, Mum"

"We're in the dining room playing Cribbage" she answered

Zain was thinking it was time he told his parents about his trip to Oz but he decided it would be better to do that later.

As he walked into the dining room he was wondering if he should tell them tonight or if he should wait a little longer to do that. His mum looked up from the game and asked, "Did you have a good time at Phillip's?

"Yep."

"Well, what did you and Phillip do?"

"We just watched The Wizard of Oz movie," he answered.

"Didn't you just watch the movie two nights ago?"

"Yep, but Phillip's never seen the movie before. I need to tell you something. It happened a year and 4 months ago and I was afraid to tell you this." Zain had decided to tell his parents just then.

His parents just looked at each other with puzzled looks.

"It all started at mass when I went to sit down in a pew and I did not think about which one I was sitting on."

His parents just looked at one another once again, then back at Zain. Zain went on, "Just as the bishop got up to speak, he turned his head and noticed me sitting in the queen's spot on the pew. He came toward me and grabbed my arm and took me to his office and the next thing I knew; I was in the Land of Oz."

"Great story son," his dad said.

"It's true!" Zain exclaimed.

Mum just smiled at him and looked down at the cards in her hand. Zain could not believe that his parents did not believe him. " Well then if you don't believe me, then how do you explain the ring with the Oz logo."

Mum looked up at Zain and replied, "You bought it from the toy store."

With anger in his eyes, Zain said, "No!! I did not! Watch I'll prove it to you! " As his parents were watching, he turned the ring twice. The next thing they knew, there was smoke and then when the smoke cleared there was no Zain.

Zain's mom looked at his dad with a look of confusion. His dad said, "Ok son, you can come out now. The joke is over. This isn't all that funny."

They both looked around, but no Zain. They both got up from the table and checked each room on the main floor. As Zain's mum was walking up the steps she heard a noise coming from the attic. She turned around and looked at her husband.

"Can you hear that noise?" she asked.

"What noise?" Just as he finished his sentence, he heard footsteps coming from the attic.

"It's coming from the attic honey! Let's go check it out." He opened the attic door slowly. As they were walking up the steps, they both heard something fall over. By the time they got to the attic, they saw nothing.

Zain's dad yelled, "Okay son, that's just about enough! Come on out now!"A couple of seconds later, two orange tabby cats came from behind a box.

"How did you both get up here?" Mrs. Tomas asked. Mr. Tomas just looked at his wife and was laughing at the way she was talking to the cats as if they were going to answer her.

She walked over and picked up the cats. Turning back around, she walked over to the steps. She bent over and set the two cats on the top step. As soon as she set them down, they bolted down the steps out of the attic.

The attic wasn't very big and it didn't have that many hiding places. After checking it out, Zain's father walked over to the small window to see if Zain had gone outside.

He was getting frustrated by now and so was Zain's mum.

She sat down on the old settee that used to be her uncle's. "Where could he be Jacob?" she asked. Jacob just looked at his wife and did not know what to say.

Chapter 20

Once again Zain was back in Oz standing outside the Emerald City door. Before he even knocked on the door, the Scarecrow came up behind him and tapped him on his shoulder.

He turned around, and it surprised him to see the Scarecrow standing there.

" Nice to see you again., Zain told the Scarecrow.

"Well, I'll be. It's been a long time since I saw you, Zain. I thought you forgot about us all after you got home and started living your old life"

"I've never forgotten this place, that's why I came back. To ask if Abigail and I could live in Emerald City or somewhere close by in Oz."

"If my memory serves me right, Abigail wanted to be a cosmetologist. But you never said what you wanted to be."

"Almost all my life I was going to military boarding school, and I had decided I wanted to serve in the British Navy. But now that I have been to Oz I have decided I would like to live here for my whole life."

"So you say. I'll need to talk to Abigail about it first. Then we shall see," the Scarecrow replied.

"I will let her know next time I write her a letter., Zain said.

"Well kid, let's not just stand out here. Let's go inside and see the others. They will be overjoyed to see you."

The Scarecrow rang the doorbell and once again I saw the same guy through the slit as last time.

"Good day Scarecrow, and I see you brought your friend Zain with you." He said.

"Well, technically, I ran into him at the door when he was about to ring the doorbell. When I saw him I tapped him on the shoulder." Scarecrow replied.

"Well, let me open the door." Slowly the door opened. It was so squeaky that it scared all of the birds that were roosting on the top of the wall surrounding the city.

Zain couldn't believe his eyes. Emerald City was brighter than it was the first time he had seen it.

Back in England, Annabel and Jacob, Zain's parents, were still in the attic worrying about Zain.

Jacob touched his wife's shoulder. She looked up at him. Jacob spoke to her in a soft voice, " There's not much we can do now, let's just go to bed. I think we will find him in his bed in the morning." he told her. They both walked out of the attic to go downstairs and head to bed. Before walking all of the way down the stairs Annabel looked back in the attic one last time to make sure that Zain wasn't really hiding and they had just missed it. When she saw nothing, she sighed and turned to finish walking down the attic steps.

Chapter 21

They woke to a car alarm going off outside, but they were too tired to even get out of bed.

They sat in their bed for about an hour and then suddenly Annabel remembered what had gone on the night before. She bolted up and reminded her husband.

They both got out of bed and slipped their robes and slippers on and walked out of their bedroom. They headed down to Zain'sbedroom to see if he was there. Jacob opened the door slowly so that if Zain was in bed then he wouldn't wake him up. He peeked around the door and saw that he was not in his bed. Annabel looked around the room and saw that in the dresser there was a pile of letters. She walked over and picked them up. When she was gone reading them, she handed them to her husband and he read them.

Nobody spoke a word. It seemed like they were sitting on the bed for a long time, but it was only 15 minutes. Jacob was the first one to speak, "Maybe Zain was telling the truth." he said to Annabel.

Annabel did not know what to say, she just looked at Jacob.

Back in Emerald City Zain was just walking around with the Scarecrow. Eventually, he remembered why he went there in the first place.

"I need to call my parents up and let them know where I'm at., he told the Scarecrow.

The Scarecrow pointed to the phone mirror and said in a soft voice, "Just touch the green button on the left side of the mirror. The operator will show up in the glass. Just give her the number and she'll put it through. If you like, you can shut the glass door for a more private conversation. After you're done, there is a red button on the right side of the mirror. Just push that button and it will end your call." He told Zain

"Thank you. " Zain replied.

When he got to the phone mirror he had to wait because someone else was using it, so he sat down on the bench and waited.

The man came out and looked at him "Hi you can use the phone mirror now." he said.

"Thank you."

After sitting down he pushed the green button. The edges of the mirror turned green and the operator came on. "The phone number, please." She said.

"I need to call 0001 (845) 696-2033 in England." Next thing he knew the phone was ringing.

In England, Zain's dad stood up and walked out of the bedroom. He went to the phone downstairs. Picking up the receiver, he said, "Hello? Hello?" No one answered. Before he put the receiver down, the mirror was lighting up. Jacob saw the two buttons on the side of it. He wasn't quite sure what they were for but he pushed the green one because it looked safe. When he pushed the green button the glass swirled for a few seconds and then all of a sudden he saw Zain through the mirror. He couldn't believe his eyes.

"ZAIN?!?" Jacob said.

"Hi, Dad. I'm here in Oz using the mirror phone." Before Zain could get a word in edgewise, his father yelled over his shoulder, "Annabel! Come quick! Zain called us through the mirror and is talking to me!!"

She ran to her husband, almost slipping on the stairs, thinking her husband had just gone crazy. When she got to the room with the phone, she saw that Zain was sitting there talking into it like it was a video call. "Zain!" She exclaimed.

"Hi, Mom. I'm here in Oz talking to you through a magic mirror that works as a phone. Here I have some people that I want you to meet." He turned around to look and see where the Scarecrow was. He saw that he was standing to the side a ways away talking to Dorothy.

With a loud voice Zain shouted out to get their attention, "Scarecrow, Dorothy, can you come here please, I have someone I want you to meet through the phone mirror." After he saw that they had heard him and started to walk over, he turned to his parents and said, "Dad, Mom, I would like you to meet the Scarecrow and Dorothy. They are two of the four people that govern and watch over Oz." He told them.

Jacob and Annabel looked at the two things (they weren't going to call the Scarecrow a person) and both said, " Nice to meet you," at the same time.

"Likewise." The Scarecrow and Dorthy replied.

They all talked for some time and then the Scarecrow told them how to call and what button to push, "But, make sure you keep the frame cover over the buttons." he told them.

"Yes, we will." they both replied.

"I'll be back around Sunday afternoon., Zain told his parents.

"See you then." his father answered.

After hanging up, Jacob and Annabel were relieved that all of what he had told them was true.

Zain visited with all of the leaders of Oz once again and talked about living in Oz someday soon.

They were all so happy that he wanted to live in Oz but there was one thing that might get in the way of him staying in Oz. The Ozma. The Ozma was the one true leading force in all of Oz. She is the one that made all of the serious decisions in Oz. And this was a kind of serious decision.

"We will have to talk to the Ozma before we decide anything. She is the one that has the say-so She could say yes or he could say no." Dorothy told Zain.

Zain looked around and asked, " Do you think she will see me today?"

The Tinman stood up, coughing before he spoke. "The only way to find out is to ask., he told Zain.

They all stood and walked over to the front door of the castle where Ozma was.

Zain raised his left hand and grabbed the door knocker. He knocked on the door three times before someone answered.

"Good day, how can I help you," asked the butler.

Zain just stood there unable to say anything.

Once again the butler asked, "How can I help you?"

This time Zain spoke up loud and clear, " I came to see Ozma?"

"May I ask who is calling?"

"Zain Thomas from England."

"Wait one minute, I'll see if she is available to see you." He walked off to go and ask Ozma if she was available to see Zain. After some time the butler came back and said, "Ozma will see you tomorrow at 10:00 am."

It upset Zain that he could not see Ozma that day. But then he thought to himself that he should probably not let anyone know that he was upset because it could get back to Ozma and she might not let him stay because of his stinky attitude. He right then decided that the next day was better than not at all.

They all talked about it and they all mutually decided that they would have Zain stay strong at Dorothy's home for the night and the remainder of his stay.

Chapter 22

Morning came, but Zain still had 3 hours left before seeing Ozma. Dorothy was still asleep in her room, so Zain decided that he was going to go back to sleep.

Just when it seemed like he was just falling asleep, Dorothy came up to him and shook him awake while saying, "Rise and shine sleepy head."

He turned over and looked at the clock. It was 7:00 am. He sat up on the side of the bed and looked up at Dorothy, "Good Morning." he said.

"I'll leave you to get dressed.b

Breakfast is downstairs. To your right where the double doors are." Dorothy told Zain.

She walked out of the bedroom and as she left; she shut the door behind her.

Zain got on his hands and knees by the bed and said a prayer asking that Ozma would let Abigail and him live in Oz soon.

He made it just in time for breakfast. He could not believe his eyes. There was so much food it was like being at a smorgasbord. Eggs, sliced ham, hash browns, bacon, cornmeal mush, orange juice, and fresh coffee. Pretty much everything anyone could want for breakfast.

"You overslept. We usually get up around 6:00" Uncle Henry told Zain. Uncle Henry was Dorothy's uncle that can to Oz to live with her. His wife, Aunt Em was also there.

"Here we eat around 7:30 to 8:00." Auntie Em Said.

Zain looked around at everyone before saying anything, "I was up at 6:00 but when I opened the bedroom door, everyone else was still asleep. I knew this because there were snoring sounds coming from both directions. I just went ahead and went back to sleep until Dorothy came and woke me up. " Zain said.

Uncle Henry spoke before Aunt Em could get a word in.

"Well, son, your problem was that you got up just a minute before the alarm went off. Why don't you go ahead and take a seat and get some breakfast? We already said grace so you can go ahead and help yourself."

Auntie Em came by with the coffeepot and poured him a cup of coffee. He said nothing to her about how he had never had coffee before because he didn't want to hurt her feelings.

He took a sip of the coffee. It tasted awful! He noticed, out of the corner of his eye, that off to the side, there was sugar and cream for the coffee. He asked Dorothy, "Can you please pass me the sugar and cream."

He put two big heaping spoonfuls of sugar and a dash of cream in his coffee. He stirred it up and took a drink. Now that there was something sweet in the bitter drink he liked it much better.

Zain was wondering if Dorothy went to school because she looked so young. So he asked her.

"So Dorthy do you go to school?"

"Yes, but school is out for the week because of apple and pear picking."

By now Aunt Em was clearing the breakfast dishes off of the table.

"Zain, let me tell you how Henry and I came to live in Oz. I was in the kitchen cooking breakfast when a cyclone hit the farm. Dorothy was out doing her morning chores along with her Uncle Henry and the hired hands when Henry yelled for me to come and help with the animals. After we got done, we all went into the cellar except Dorothy. We had no clue where she was. About a week after the cyclone hit we had finally given up all hope of ever seeing Dorothy ever again.

One day, out of nowhere, I heard my name being shouted over and over again. I stood up and looked around and coming over the hill was Dorothy."

"But that does not tell me how you came to live in Oz," Zain said

"Hush! Let me finish." Aunt Em exclaimed. "Back to what I was saying. When Dorothy came back all she could talk about was Oz. Eventually, we had to tell her no more talking about this made-up place called Oz. We thought she had just gone crazy and had a make-believe friend. A couple of years later we were sitting around the kitchen table playing cards, just the three of us. A gust of wind came under the kitchen door and startled the cat. Next, we hear the shutters moving. Henry got up and looked out the window. Coming from over the hill was another cyclone!"

"It was too late for us to make a run to the cellar. The house started moving and we could feel the house spinning. We all went under the table holding on to each other for dear life. In just a few minutes, the house came down with a loud thump. We all came out from under the table and strolled to the kitchen door. Henry opened the door and to our surprise, we saw the Tinman and Scarecrow walking down the yellow brick road."

" Henry and I just looked at each other and said plainly, 'We must be in Oz'. Dorothy was so happy she ran out of the house and to the Tinman and Scarecrow. 'Dorothy I'm so happy to see you again,' said Tinman. 'Likewise,' said the Scarecrow. Dorothy obviously could not hold in her excitement. She told the two that they needed to come and meet us. When they came over to meet us, I couldn't believe my eyes. I just chuckled and told the that I didn't think that they were even real until that moment. They asked us how we had gotten there and we told them about the cyclone. We also told them that we and nothing to go back to. The bank was going to foreclose on the farm anyway and now the cyclone had destroyed it. They asked us if we wanted to go ahead and live here and we immediately said yes." Aunt Em took a breath before she continued.

" Ozma knew that we were restless by the time we had been here for a month. We had no farm to keep us busy and Dorothy had school and she was always going something with her friends. So she appointed Henry as Keeper of the Jewel in Oz and to keep all jewels polished and to make sure the jewels were not stolen. I was appointed stocking." Before Auntie

Em could say another word Zain asked, "What do you mean by you were appointed stocking?"

"I was just getting to that part when you interrupted me! It means I am to take care of all of the stockings that have holes in them and make new ones to sell. We live in a kitty corner outside of Emerald City. We used to live in Emerald City but we wanted our place to call home. We still work in Emerald City and love our jobs and I still raise chickens as I did back in Kansas. After some time here, Ozma asked if all three of us would like to live in Oz forever.

So we all said yes," Em finished.

Chapter 23

Zain said little on the walk to Emerald City. He wasn't sure what Ozma would say.

The Scarecrow rang the doorbell and once again they were inside the Emerald City.

There were so many activities going on it was hard to see everything.

As they were walking up the steps a little redheaded girl came up to Zain.

"Are you Dorothy's brother?"

"No. Just a friend," he answered.

He knocked on the door it seemed like forever before the butler opened the door.

"Glad to see you came back. Ozma is waiting for you in the library. I'll take you to her." he said and then he turned around to lead us to the library.

The door slammed behind us before we followed the butler. Zain couldn't believe how big the castle was. He also couldn't wait to find out Ozma's answer.

It was a long walk from the front door to the library but they finally made it. It made Zain very happy to finally be where Ozma could answer his question. When the Ozma turned around Zain took a sharp breath in surprise. Ozma was a lot younger than Zain would have thought that she was.

"So you are the young man that wants to live in Oz." She said matter-of-factly.

Zain took a deep breath "Yes, ma'am, I sure do. Along with a young lady that I want to marry and live here with her. She wants to live here too."

"Tell me, why should I let you live in Oz?"

"When I first came here I wasn't sure about the places in Oz, but I found out most of the people and animals are very nice and friendly here. Not like where Abigail I come from," he replied.

"If you don't mind me asking, where are you both from?" Ozma asked.

"I'm from England and Abigail is from the United States. " He answered.

"Well, If we can get a hold of Abigail today and she lets me know why she wants to live here then maybe I'll say yes. Let's go to my phone mirror. Follow me."

We all followed her straight down to the end of the hallway where the phone mirror hung on the wall.

"Do you have her phone number?" Ozma asked Zain.

He took his cell phone out of the front pocket of his jeans and went to his contacts.

"Wait one minute while I get the operator." She said and gave Zain's small smile. She pressed the green button on the side of the mirror and the operator showed up on the glass.

"Number please." the operator said.

Ozma looked at the phone number on the screen of the cell phone and read it off, "1-(541) 405-1110." She told the operator.

I was the only one home because I had a cold and Mom would not let me go to church. I was sitting on my bunkbed crocheting when a bright green light shot out of my mirror. I was already startled by the green light but to make matters worse there appears a green face from the mirror. And then it started talking to me.

"Operator. You've got a call from Ozma." The operator told me.

At first, I did not know what to think. I almost fell off the top bunk. Lucky for me, I grabbed hold of the railing to keep from falling. Then I jumped down to the floor. I stood in front of the mirror and just looked at it because I did not know what else to say. I was speechless.

"Got a phone call for Abigail." the operator said again.

"I'm Abigail," I said.

"I'll connect you now." I stood there waiting to see what Ozma looked like. I had heard of Ozma but I had never met her before or ever even seen what she looked like.

As I looked at the mirror, two faces showed up on the glass. It was Zain and who I guessed was Princess Ozma. "Zain is that you?" I asked him. I just couldn't believe that it was him standing there on the other side of the mirror.

"Sure is, and I would like you to meet the Princess of Oz."

I bowed to the Princess of Oz. "It's very nice to meet you," I told her.

"Zain told me you would like to live in Oz. Can you tell me why?" she asked me.

"Ever since I was a little girl I always wanted to live in Oz. After I read all the books and seen the movies more than a dozen times it couldn't leave my mind. The thought of living here at least. When my two siblings came to Oz I was so jealous and then I got to come and it was a dream come true. I also really like the landscape and people in Oz." I told her.

"Well, what type of job would you do in Oz, if I may ask," she asked me.

"I would like to be a cosmetology and become a beautician," I replied.

"So I guess you don't have your degree in cosmetology yet?" she asked with a small smile.

"No," I told her returning the smile.

"So Zain, you did not tell me what type of job you would like to do in Oz," she said, turning toward Zain.

"I have been in military school since I was in the 6th grade and my dream was to be in the Navy in England, but now that I have been to Oz I would like to join the Oz Navy if you guys have one." He told Ozma.

"Abigail, where do you plan on going to college," Ozma asked me.

"I thought if it was okay, I could go to the college in Oz," I told her.

I saw that Ozma was thinking it through for a minute before saying anything.

"Well, you can go to college here under one condition. That you can only see your family twice a year. I will give you the recommendation to go to college here and you need to get a job at one of the coffee shops until you graduate. Then you can open up your shop." she told me.

Zain piped up and asked, "Can I build our cabin in between Brewerville and the college?"

"I will give you both permission to live in the land of Oz. You and your children and their children etc. But you both must finish school. I will give your family a special button that sticks on any mirror and only they can use it to talk to you, but it will have to wait until you finish school. And you can get married in Oz." she told the both of us.

We both agreed to the terms. We said our goodbyes. I had 3 years of school left and Zain had two years left.

After that phone call, we both wrote letters to each other monthly and we stayed in touch. Even though we had a lot of time still until our schooling was done we still held on to the hope of seeing each other soon. Time ticked by slower than we ever thought that it ever could but we held in there. Even if it didn't seem like it was ever going to happen we both knew that it would. Sooner than we thought.

Keep your eyes open for the next Family of Oz book, Meadowfoam of Oz. Also, look out for Abigail Returns to Oz Book 7 of the Family of Oz series.

Don't miss out!

Visit the website below and you can sign up to receive emails whenever Josie Ann Tyler publishes a new book. There's no charge and no obligation.

https://books2read.com/r/B-A-LPGM-AHWHC

BOOKS 2 READ

Connecting independent readers to independent writers.

Also by Josie Ann Tyler

Family of Oz series
Jigsaw Puzzle of Oz
Hairdresser Of Oz

Standalone
Kingdome Blown To Unknown Part Of Oz
Farmer Boy Of Oz The First Book In The Family Of Oz series